LOGANSPORT LIBRARY
D1191415

LITTLE BROWN BEAR
Takes a Bath

Written by Claude Lebrun
Illustrated by Danièle Bour

Children's Press®
A Division of Grolier Publishing
New York London Hong Kong Sydney
Danbury, Connecticut

Little Brown Bear
likes to take a bath.
The water feels
warm and good.

He likes to play
with toy animals
in the water.
He has a turtle,
a frog, a goldfish,
and a duck.

Little Brown Bear
fills a plastic bottle
with water.
It makes bubbles.
He likes to hear
the sounds it makes.

Little Brown Bear
pours the water
from the bottle.
It splashes.
He likes to hear
the sounds it makes.

Little Brown Bear
holds on
to the sides of the tub.
He leans back
in the water.
It makes big waves.

Little Brown Bear
rubs soap
on his hands
and washes himself.
He likes to feel clean.

Papa Bear comes in.
"Time to dry off,
Little Brown Bear,"
he says.
"Now you are nice
and clean!"

This series was produced by Mijo Beccaria.

The illustrations were created by Danièle Bour.

The text was written by Claude Lebrun and edited by Pomme d'Api.

English translation by Children's Press.

ISBN 0-516-07842-9 (School & Library Edition)
ISBN 0-516-17842-3 (Trade Edition)
ISBN 0-516-17804-0 (Boxed Set)
Library of Congress information on file.

A Division of Grolier Publishing, Sherman Turnpike, Danbury, Connecticut
Originally published in French by Bayard.

Published simultaneously in Canada.
Printed in Belgium
1 2 3 4 5 6 7 8 9 00 R 05 04 03 02 01 00 99 98 97 96